LIFE EDUCATION

Me and my World

Written by
Alexandra Parsons

Illustrated by
Teri Gower and Stuart Harrison

FRANKLIN WATTS
A DIVISION OF GROLIER PUBLISHING
NEW YORK ● LONDON ● HONG KONG ● SYDNEY
DANBURY, CONNECTICUT

First American Edition
© 1996 by Franklin Watts
A Division of Grolier Publishing
Sherman Turnpike
Danbury, Connecticut 06816

10 9 8 7 6 5 4 3 2 1
Parsons, Alexandra.
  Me and my world / by Alexandra Parsons.
  p. cm. — (Life education)
  Includes index.
  Summary: Discusses the importance of treating
others as you would like to be treated, covering
such areas of unacceptable behavior as stealing and
hurting the feelings of those who are different from
you.
  ISBN 0-531-14375-9 (lib. bdg.)
  1. Ethics — Juvenile literature. 2. Children —
Conduct of life.
  [1. Conduct of life. 2. Ethics.] I. Title. II.
Series.
BJ1631.P37 1995
170 — dc20   95-37521
                              CIP AC

Edited by: Janet De Saulles and Helen Lanz
Designed by: Sally Boothroyd
Commissioned photography by: Steve Shott
Illustrations by: Teri Gower and Stuart
Harrison

Acknowledgments:
Commissioned photography by Steve Shott: title
page; contents page; 6, 7, 8, 10, 13, 14, 16, 27, 29.
Researched photographs: David Hoffman 19;
Associated Press 23 (right); Hulton Deutsch 23
(left); Science Photo library 25.
Artwork: Cover illustrations by John Shackell.
Cartoon illustrations of "alien" by Stuart Harrison.
All other cartoon illustrations by Teri Gower.

The Publisher and Life Education International are
indebted to Vince Hatton and Laurie Noffs for their
invaluable help.

The Publisher would like to extend special thanks to
all the actors who appear in the
Life Education books (Key Stage 2):

Jessamy Heath	Danny Mancini
Dishni Payagale Don	Peter Wood
Young-min Kim	Stephen Miles
Debbie Okangi	Daisy Doodles
Michael Wood	Joseph Wood
Mark Wall	Simon Wall
Andrew Wall	Christopher Wall
Vanessa Neita	Amber Neita-Crowley
Jun King	Ken King
Ben Clewley	

"*Each second we live is a new and unique moment of the universe, a moment that will never be again....And what do we teach our children? We teach them that two and two make four and that Paris is the capital of France.*

When will we also teach them: do you know who you are? You are a marvel. You are unique. In all the years that have passed, there has never been another child like you. And look at your body – what a wonder it is! Your legs, your arms, your clever fingers, the way you move. You may become a Shakespeare, a Michelangelo, a Beethoven. You have the capacity for anything. Yes, you are a marvel. And when you grow up, can you then harm another who is, like you, a marvel? You must cherish one another. You must work – we must all work – to make this world worthy of its children."

Pablo Casals

Hi everybody! The name is Zapp. I'm from Pluto – you know, turn left past Saturn and you can't miss it. Just popped over to check you all out!

CONTENTS

. . YOU CAN MAKE A DIFFERENCE .

Our world is full of possibilities. It is full of wonderful things, and the most wonderful of all are its people – ordinary everyday people like you. People can have a tremendous influence on us. Their effect on others can be good or bad, or somewhere in between. And every single one of us can make a difference to someone else.

I gave my mom a big kiss and told her how much I love her.

You know, it really cheered me up.

I helped my kid brother with his homework.

I think it's really cool having a big sister...

I telephoned my grandmother; she's a little deaf and you have to shout, so it's not easy.

That's my grandson. He phoned me this morning, the little lamb. It made my day.

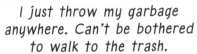

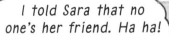

. . . . NICE OR NASTY? . . . . . .

Everyone has feelings. And feelings can get hurt. Some people get a kick out of making other people unhappy; this is not only unkind – it's just plain mean. Why is it that some people behave in a nicer way than others? People who think about good and bad are called philosophers, and over the years they have come up with some interesting theories.

Babies know nothing of good or bad; they become what they are through experience.

Goodness is always good, even if no one knows about it.

Goodness is judged according to the number of people who benefit from it.

All people are born good; badness is something they learn.

Everyone has the same right to happiness.

You should only do the kind of things you wouldn't mind other people doing.

The debate goes on...

WHY PEOPLE BULLY

Bullying is not kind. Bullies are usually people who find it difficult to make friends, so they try to find another way to attract attention. They usually pick on easy targets – people who are different in some way or who are easy to make fun of – and make their lives miserable. They think this makes them look cool, and it usually attracts a bunch of other insecure people who like to be seen as part of a "gang" or clique.

Some people can be unkind to others in order to make themselves look "cool" (left). How do you think you would feel if you were the one being excluded (far right)?

Have you got the money? Gimme your lunch box, maggot!

Please don't hit me! Watch my glasses! Here, just take it.

Did you enjoy your lunch, Martin?

Yes, thanks. Mom – I want to learn karate!!

Why do you think Martin didn't tell his mom what was happening to him at school?

ARE BULLIES HAPPY PEOPLE?

Silly, Sally! Silly, Sally! S-s-silly!

I I c-c-an't h-h-help it . P-p-please l-l-leave m-m-e al-lone.

I don't know. She just seemed so goofy. It makes the other girls laugh when I tease her.

I can't believe you've been harrasing that poor girl. Why do you do that Mandy?

Go on, say "silly Sally," silly, say it loud.

S-s-s-silly, S-s-s-ally...

Mandy, is anything wrong at school?

Oh, Mom, it was so hard changing schools in the middle of a term. I miss my old friends.... No one even noticed me until I started pushing Sally around... but they're not REAL friends, they're just frightened of me. I'm so miserable.

You're lucky! On Pluto, we have computers to tell us how to behave. You can each make up your own minds, maybe that's what makes you all so interesting....

Do you think it made Mandy feel good to make Sally unhappy?

. . . . CLOSED MINDS . . . .

Some people have made up their minds that they only like things they know about. And they think they can tell what everyone and everything is like just by looking. This is called prejudice. Prejudice means judging on appearances, before you know the facts.

THE OPEN MIND CHALLENGE

Most people who are prejudiced are frightened of difference and change. Try to imagine a world in which everybody is just the same. A world in which all the people like the same things, speak the same way, are good at the same things, and bad at the same things. They sing the same songs, dance the same dances, and eat the same food.

If everyone looked the same and wanted the same things, life would be dull.

CELEBRATING DIFFERENCES

We are all different, our families are different, and our experiences are different. It is good that people like doing different things. We learn from one another and our own lives are made more interesting if we meet people who think in different ways, or have different likes and dislikes, and different ways of doing things.

Being different is fun!

SOME REALLY SILLY WAYS TO FIND OUT WHAT PEOPLE ARE LIKE

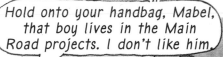

. . . . . AMREEN AND ANNIE . . . . .

THE STORY OF A FRIENDSHIP: FINDING OUT ABOUT EACH OTHER

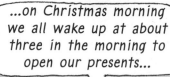

...on Christmas morning we all wake up at about three in the morning to open our presents...

...on the festival of Diwali we light millions of candles...

That sounds fun!

Mom, this is Amreen and her parents.

Oh!

I can't believe it Mom, you were so rude!

You see, just as I thought, those people have no respect.

Those people? What do you mean, *those people?* You didn't even say hello!

They have funny food.

I've tried it. It's delicious.

They have a different religion.

And that makes them not worth knowing?

Today we are going to talk about prejudice. Prejudice means judging people before you get to know them. Making up your mind before you know the facts. Can anyone think of someone who is prejudiced?

My mom and dad!

Sometimes kids have the right instinct. Will you remember that when you grow up?

.. OTHER PEOPLE'S PROPERTY ...

Can it ever be right to steal something from somebody else or to destroy their property? Maybe people wouldn't steal or vandalize if they stopped for a minute to think what it feels like to be on the receiving end.

MAKING EXCUSES
Some people might think that stealing from stores isn't bad because they are not taking from a person. But if that store belonged to you, you might feel differently about it.

STAYING IN BUSINESS

We'll close for the day and add up the money.

We need to order some more stock. We're very low on pens and pencils.

I don't believe it! It's happened again! According to the stock sheets we should have sold $150 worth of goods, but there's only $75 in the register.

I'll have to mark the prices up. I can't afford to pay your wages if it goes on like this. I can barely afford the rent.

So I'm out of a job, am I? That's great!

SOME MONTHS LATER

Shame it closed down. Now we have to walk all the way to Main Street.

I stole heaps of stuff from that store! I wonder why it closed.

WHY VANDALISE?

It can be very upsetting to find your things smashed or ruined. It seems so pointless, just spoiling something because it isn't yours. Maybe people do it because they feel jealous, or perhaps just because they want people to know they exist, or then again, it may be their idea of having a good time. What do you think?

THE HOMECOMING

Who lives here?

No idea! Let's have some fun!

Yeah! That was great!

Picture their faces when they get home! Ha! Ha! Come on, let's go!

Hey! Look what some bonehead's done to our house! That's totally uncool.

Oh NO! My computer! My CD Rom drive!

I'm really bummed! To think that someone's been around here while we were out... destroying our things...

I'll never be able to afford another computer!

Well, it's hard to feel sorry for them!

.... OLLIE AND THE APPLES ....

TWO POINTS OF VIEW

Well, you could always try asking for it back.

What's the point, Mom? He never gives them back to me. You try.

Well, he didn't mean to kick it into your garden, Mr. Grizzle.

That's as may be. He did, though, and he's not getting it back.

But it's his ball, Mr. Grizzle. He bought it with his own pocket money. You can't just take it.

That ball entered my garden unlawfully. I know my rights. Good day, madam. Be off with you! You're trespassing on my land.

Stop! Thief!

This is an outrage. The police chief's a good friend! I know my rights.

This young rascal trespassed on my land and stole my apples! Am I pressing charges? Of course I'm pressing charges! Lock the little troublemaker up!

But he's stolen two soccer balls, one Frisbee, and three tennis balls...

Shush, Ollie.

It's a fact of life that balls go over garden walls, sir, and as I see it, although you have every right to hang onto them, I don't think you should. As for you, young man, you shouldn't have done what you did, either. Mr. Grizzle, would you kindly return the assorted collection of projectiles belonging to young Ollie here? Ollie, would you return the apples to Mr. Grizzle? That's settled then! Thank you sir, madam, good day!

Yucch! These apples are as sour as their owner. It seems to me Ollie didn't mean any harm, but it's a good thing he gave the apples back.

15

**I WANT,
I WANT,
I WANT**

I want a car like that.

I want that outfit.

I want that dog.

I want those stickers.

Those of you who have brought in the money for the class trip, give it to the school secretary after morning recess.

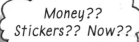

Money?? Stickers?? Now??

16

But my dad gave me that wallet for my birthday, and it took me weeks to save the money for the class trip and now it's all gone!

If anyone knows anything about what happened to Amy's wallet, they could just leave something in my desk during lunchtime and nothing more will be said.

I can get those stickers today.

Go on Maude, give it back. You can buy those stickers any time with your own pocket money. Don't be mean.

It's no use, she's not listening.

Well, mean old Maude. I wonder what kind of person she'll grow up to be? Not my type, I think.

17

. . . . . RULES, RULES, RULES! . . . . .

E ven when you grow up, people are still telling you what to do. Don't walk on the grass! No parking! Don't drop litter! Pay your taxes! Send your children to school! It is because people expect to have rights that rules, or laws, are made to protect those rights.

YOUR RIGHT TO CARE

You have the right to expect to grow up safely, in a loving family. In order to protect those rights, there are laws preventing people from abusing or mistreating children. There are also laws preventing children from being sent out to work, and from being left on their own.

My dad's always beating up me and my mom. I can't stand it anymore.

You don't have to put up with that.

Just dial the ChildLine at 1-800-555-1111. There are people there who can help you.

YOUR RIGHT TO EDUCATION

You have the right to knowledge. Schools have rules to prevent distractions and disruptions in class so that children can learn properly.

Rome is the capital city of Italy, and Athens is the capital of Greece.

Stop that at once! Turn that thing OFF! Get back to your seats!

Now she's got time to teach us something instead of yelling at those two all day.

YOUR RIGHT TO PROTECTION FROM YOURSELF!

Children don't always know what is best for them, so there are laws stopping people from selling them guns, alcohol, drugs, and other dangerous substances. Makes sense, doesn't it?

Let's go get some cigarettes!

I'm sorry, son. I'm not allowed to sell cigarettes to minors. It's the law.

'Mean old Maude and the others haven't got away with their evil deeds after all . . .

You're finished! You should be ashamed of yourselves, acting this way in a children's book.

YOUR RIGHT TO OWN THINGS

You have a right to keep the things you own. There are laws to protect property and people who are caught stealing or vandalizing have to face the fact that they have broken the law.

But what about all the bullies? Why isn't there a law stopping people from being nasty?

Sometimes people have to do a number of hours helping out in their community to make up for breaking the law.

19

.... JUST IMAGINE ....

Imagine for a moment that you are the **A**bsolute **S**upreme **N**umero **U**no **R**uler **O**f **T**he **U**niverse. Nice thought, isn't it? It is your job to come up with a brand-new rule book for the world. You want to be popular with the people, which means not too many laws, and yet you want to make life run smoothly for everybody. This could be tricky.

OVER TO YOU, ASNUROTU!

Um...

Your Supremeness, the world is waiting...

Um.... There will be no laws, no rules, no order, no money. People can just ... er... do their own thing. They should like that!

As your Supremeness wishes...

Hurrah! LONG LIVE ASNUROTU!

A few weeks later...

THE WHOLE TEAM'S OFFSIDE! BRING BACK THE RULE BOOK! WHERE'S THE REF?

Who's winning?

Dunno. I'm leaving. It's no fun now that there aren't any rules.

Meanwhile, at a local supermarket

AAAAARRGGHHH!

I saw it first!

Gimme!

It's mine!

I'm emigrating to another planet. I can't run a store without money and order books and carts and staff and lunch breaks and opening times. Wait till I get my hands on that imbecile Asnurotu ...

THE RULE OF ABSOLUTE SUPREME NUMERO UNO RULER OF THE UNIVERSE (known to his mom and dad as Tim)

ASNUROTU Tim's reign began with a wild burst of enthusiasm. Everyone admired his determination to get rid of the millions of boring rules that got in the way of people having fun. However, what Tim didn't realize (and his courtiers and advisers didn't tell him) was that the only people to benefit from having no rules were the bullies. There was no one to take care of the sick or the old or the very young and no one to drive the buses or collect the garbage. Everyone wanted to be a movie star. Tim's time in power was an absolute disaster for everyone and he was lucky to escape with his life.

. . . WHEN RULES GO WRONG . . .

H istory has many examples of single-minded leaders who were convinced they had the perfect master plan for governing the world. They didn't always start out being wrong, but certainly ended up that way.

When I grow up, I want to be in charge, because I know what's best. I know that people like me should be in power, and the riffraff should be slaves and servants.

How can you say such things! In my ideal society, everyone will be equal, and share everything. I know I can make it work.

MANY YEARS LATER. . .

We can't have the riffraff reading books and newspapers that give them ideas! Next thing we know they'll be taking our jobs and marrying our daughters. Ban the books! Ban the newspapers!

But the comrade farmers have got to stay on the farms producing food. It is in the plan. They can't go having ideas about freedom of choice! What have they been reading?

SOME YEARS LATER

Those people are just a burden on our economy! Get rid of them! I don't care how, just get rid of them!

We cannot let people think they have rights to think as they please, it will ruin everything! The people must do as they are told. Get rid of the troublemakers, I don't care how! Just get rid of them!

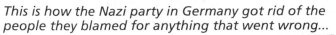

This is how the Nazi party in Germany got rid of the people they blamed for anything that went wrong...

...and this is how the Chinese Communist party dealt with students who wanted freedom to choose the way they lived their lives.

You stand for everything I despise.

Well, boys, you turned out to be as bad as each other. You may have started out with different ideals, but in the end, you were equally desperate to stop people from speaking out for personal freedom.

The world should never forget what can happen when people with extreme views get into power.

. . . . . A PERFECT WORLD . . . . .

I t is easy to criticize other people's attempts to lay down a plan for society. The truth is that a perfect society needs perfect people and no one is perfect! Some people are greedier than others, and some people are just mad and bad. You can't change the way people behave toward one another without laws and rules. Think about how you might make a perfect world.

IMAGINE... NO MONEY...

Long ago, there was no money. In many societies people traded goods and services. This system is called a barter system and it could work quite well. It would certainly teach people the real value of things, but would they be prepared to pay those kind of prices?

IMAGINE... NO POSSESSIONS

It sounds like a good idea, but only if everyone could be content just with what they needed: a change of clothes, a roof over their heads, a book to read, music to listen to, a meal on the table... but then no two people have the same needs..

IMAGINE... NO WORK

Again, it sounds appealing but.... A lot of people enjoy going to work; they like the people they meet there; they enjoy working as a team; or they find what they do fulfilling. People like to be together, and do things together.

IMAGINE... NO SCHOOL

There must be times when you've thought this would be a terrific plan. But think what it would be like if you didn't know anything, if you couldn't do math, or read, or write. Where would you meet your friends and make new ones? And would you ever feel that nice glow you get when you've done something really well?

MAKE THE WORLD A BETTER PLACE

magine your actions as being like stones you throw into a pond. The ripples keep rippling long after the stone has sunk to the bottom. Think of the pond as your world and the ripples as the effects of your actions. If you throw in something pleasant or constructive, you're going to send out good ripples, and if you toss in something mean or thoughtless, the people around you will get bad ripples. Imagine the state of the pond if every ripple was a bad one!

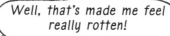

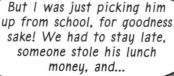

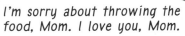

When was the last time you cleaned up? Helping others makes the world a better place. Even chores can be fun!

. . . CARING FOR OUR PLANET . . .

People are not made to exist alone. We all need one another. That is why it is important to care about other people, not just the people nearest to us, but people all over the world. We can make a difference in the lives of people on the other side of the world by raising money for charity or by refusing to buy things that exploit their environment. We can do our part to take care of future generations, too, by making sure we take care of our planet properly.

LETTER FROM LIFE EDUCATION

Dear Friends:

The first Life Education Center was opened in Sydney, Australia, in 1979. Founded by the Rev. Ted Noffs, the Life Education program came about as a result of his many years of work with drug addicts and their families.

Ted Noffs realized that preventive education, beginning with children from the earliest possible age all the way into their teenage years, was the only long-term solution to drug abuse and other related problems, including violence and AIDS.

Life Education pioneered the use of technology in a futuristic "Classroom of the 21st Century," designed to show in an exciting way the beauty of life on planet Earth and how drugs including nicotine and alcohol can destroy the delicate balance of human life itself. In every Life Education classroom, there are electronic displays that show the major body systems including the respiratory, nervous, digestive, and immune systems. There is a talking brain and wondrous star ceiling. And there is Harold the Giraffe who appears in many of the programs and is Life Education's official mascot. Programs start in preschool and go all the way through high school.

There are parents' programs and violence prevention classes. Life Education has also begun to create interactive software for home and school computers as well as having its own home page on the Internet, the global information superhighway (the address is http://www.lec.org/).

There are Life Education Centers operating in seven countries (Thailand, the United States, the United Kingdom, New Zealand, Australia, Hong Kong, and New Guinea).

This series of books will allow the wonder and magic of Life Education to reach many more young people with the simple message that each human being is special and unique and that in all of the past, present, and future history there will never be another person exactly the same as you.

If you would like to learn more about Life Education International, contact us at one of the addresses listed below or, if you have a computer with a modem, you can write to Harold the Giraffe at Harold@lec.org and you'll find out a giraffe can send E-mail!

Let's learn to live.

All of us at the Life Education Center.

Life Education, USA
149 Addison Ave
Elmhurst, Illinois
60126
Tel: 708-530-8999
Fax: 708-530-7241

Life Education, UK
20 Long Lane
London
EC1A 9HL
United Kingdom
Tel: 0171-600-6969
Fax: 0171-600-6979

Life Education,
Australia
29 Hughes Street
Potts Point
NSW 2011
Australia
Tel: 0061-2-358-2466
Fax: 0061-2-357-2569

Life Education,
New Zealand
126 The Terrace
PO Box 10-769
Wellington
New Zealand
Tel: 0064-4-472-9620
Fax: 0064-4-472-9609

GLOSSARY

Barter Exchanging goods and services without using money.

Christmas The Christian festival that each year celebrates the birth of Christ on December 25.

Communist A member of the Communist party. Communism is a political system developed in the 20th century in which all property is owned by the state and everyone works for, and is paid by, the state.

Diwali An important Hindu festival held each year between September and November. It is often called the Festival of Light because the lighting of candles is an important part of the celebrations.

Economy This can have several meanings: being careful with money or resources; something cheap, for example, economy-class fares or economy-size toothpaste; or the wealth and resources of a country.

Environment Our surroundings, wherever we live in the world: homes, streets, playgrounds, parks, countryside, woods, forests, rivers, seas, and so on.

Karate A form of unarmed combat using the feet and hands as weapons. It was developed in Japan.

Nazi party The German National Socialist party of which Adolf Hitler became the leader in the 1930s. A hatred of certain races and religions was a feature of the party.

Philosopher Someone who studies ideas and thinks about human behavior and the meaning of life.

Pluto The outermost planet of the known solar system.

Prejudice An opinion, usually unpleasant, held by someone who knows little about the subject or person concerned.

Trespass To go onto land or into a property that does not belong to you without permission.

Vandal Someone who deliberately destroys or damages someone else's property or belongings.

FURTHER INFORMATION

American Civil Liberties Union
132 West 43rd Street
New York, NY 10036
Telephone: 212-944-9800
Fax: 212-354-5290

Children's Alliance for the Protection of the Environment
P.O. Box 307
Austin, TX 78767
Telephone: 512-476-2273
Fax: 512-476-2301

Citizens for a Better America
P.O. Box 356
Halifax, VA 24558
Telephone: 804-476-7757

National Committee for the Prevention of Child Abuse
332 S. Michigan Avenue
Suite 1600
Chicago, IL 60604
Telephone: 312-663-3520
Fax: 312-939-8962

INDEX